For Rory and Orla,

the sweetest cups of tea —B.F.

For Dennis —D.W.

G. P. PUTNAM'S SONS
An imprint of Penguin Random House LLC, New York

Visit us online at penguinrandomhouse.com

Library of Congress Cataloging-in-Publication Data
Names: Ferry, Beth, author. | Wulfekotte, Dana, illustrator.
Title: Tea time / Beth Ferry; illustrated by Dana Wulfekotte. | Other titles: Tee time
Description: New York: G. P. Putnam's Sons, [2021]
Summary: When Grampy invites Frannie to tee off with him at the golf course,
Frannie and her mother misunderstand and pack a picnic basket for a lovely tea time.
Identifiers: LCCN 2020048758 (print) | LCCN 2020048759 (ebook)
ISBN 9781524741082 (hardcover) | ISBN 9781524741082 (ebook) | ISBN 9781524741112 (kindle edition)
Subjects: CYAC: Grandparent and child—Fiction. | Grandfathers—Fiction. | Golf—Fiction. | Afternoon teas—Fiction.
Classification: LCC PZ7.1.F47 Tc 2021 (print) | LCC PZ7.1.F47 (ebook) | DDC [E]—dc23
LC record available at https://lccn.loc.gov/2020048758
LC ebook record available at https://lccn.loc.gov/2020048759

Manufactured in China by RR Donnelley Asia Printing Solutions Ltd.
ISBN 9781524741082 | 10 9 8 7 6 5 4 3 2 1

Design by Nicole Rheingans | Text set in ITC Leawood Std
The art was rendered in graphite and colored digitally.

Tea Time

Story by
Beth Ferry

Pictures by
Dana Wulfekotte

putnam

G. P. PUTNAM'S SONS

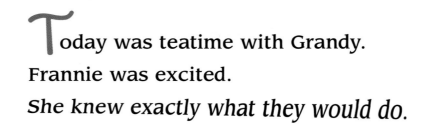

Today was teatime with Grandy.

Frannie was excited.

She knew exactly what they would do.

Today was tee time with Frannie.

Grandy was excited.

He knew exactly what they would do.

Frannie's mother helped her pack the picnic basket.

In went:

teacups and saucers,
small matching plates,
a thermos filled with hot tea,
peanut butter and jelly sandwiches,
and two slices of chocolate cake.

Chocolate cake was Grandy's favorite.

Her mother folded a soft blue blanket
for the picnic.

"Teatime at the park
with your grandfather.
How lovely," she said.

At the same time, Grandy was packing his gear.

In went:

golf balls,
golf clubs,
golf shoes,
sunblock,
and bug spray.

Frannie hated bugs!

"Golfing at Quail Ridge with Frannie. How lovely," Grammy said.

Grandy picked Frannie up, tick-tock on time.

"Ready?" Grandy asked. "Our tee time is at two."

"Tea for two," said Frannie.

They drove past beautiful fields of green.

"So pretty," Frannie said.

"Isn't it?" Grandy agreed. "I love Quail Ridge."

"Will there be quails?"

"I don't think so," said Grandy.
"But I'm counting on
a lot of birdies."

"Will there be swings?"

"Lots and lots of swinging,"
Grandy said. "Don't worry.
I'll teach you."

"Grandy!" Frannie laughed.

"I already know how to swing."

"A thousand pardons.

I didn't know you'd played before."

"I play every day, Grandy.

It's what I do."

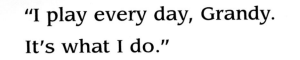

When they arrived at Quail Ridge,
Frannie ran onto the freshly cut field.

She spread out the blanket,
placed some daisies in a cup,
and unpacked the picnic basket.

"It's time for tea!" Frannie called to Grandy.

"It's time to tee off,"
Grandy called to Frannie.

"FORE!"

A golf ball crashed
directly onto the blanket.

Tea was splashed.

Sandwiches were smashed.

Cake was crushed.

Grandy rushed to help.

"Our teatime is ruined!"
Frannie wailed.

"Not by a long shot,"
Grandy said.

He brought her to the clubhouse and told the host, "Tea for two!"

Grandy and Frannie had tea:
hot tea in china cups
with club sandwiches and
chocolate chip cookies.

It was tea-lightful!

Later, Grandy watched Frannie watch the golfers.

"Want to give it a whirl?" he asked.

"We'll start small," he added.

"A hole in one!" Frannie exclaimed,
jumping up and down. "I got a hole in one!"

"Frannie, my girl," Grandy said, laughing.
"I do believe golf just may be . . .

. . . your cup of tea."

GOLF TERMS

birdie: a score of one under par on a hole

chip: a shot designed to roll farther than it flies

eagle: a score of two under par on a hole

fore: shouted by a golfer as a warning when it appears possible that a ball may hit other players or spectators

par: the score an expert golfer would be expected to make on a hole

slice: a golf shot that curves hard to the right

swing: to make a stroke with the golf club in your hands

tee: the start of the golf hole, where the first shot is taken; also a small piece of equipment—made of wood or plastic—placed in the ground that the golf ball is placed upon prior to the first stroke on a hole

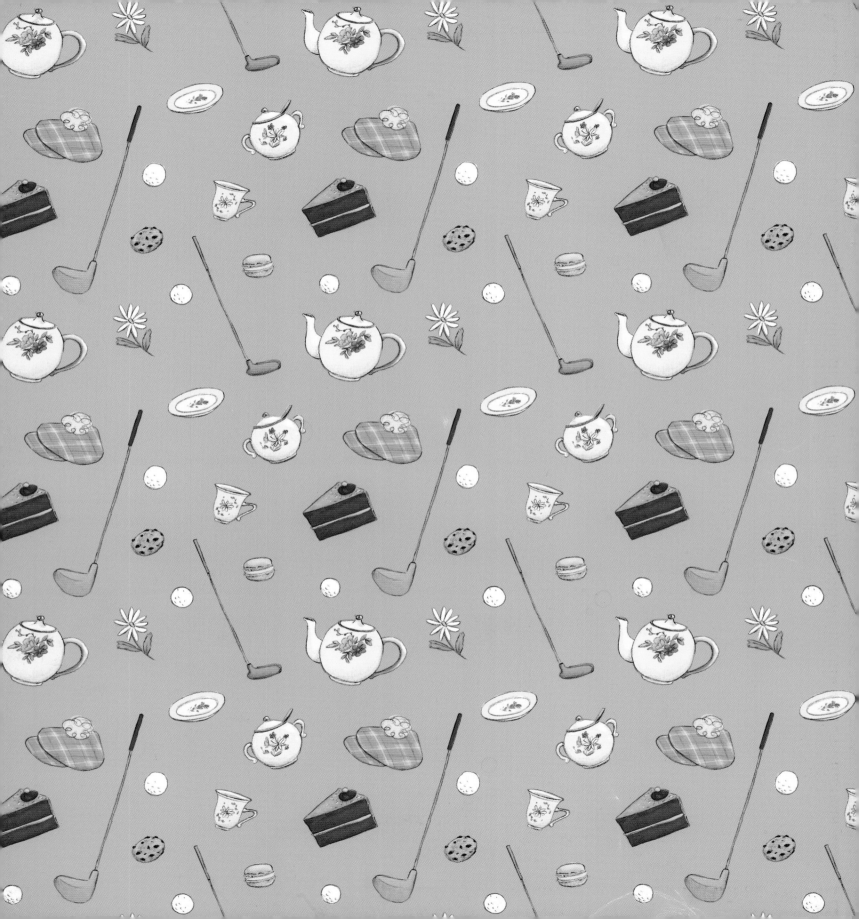